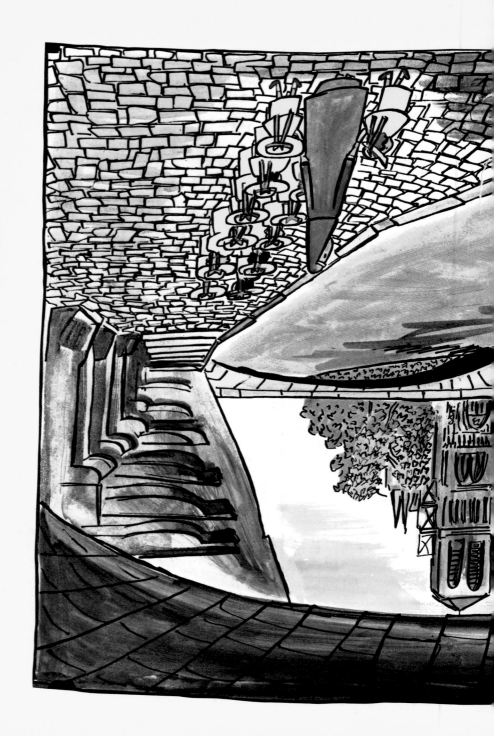

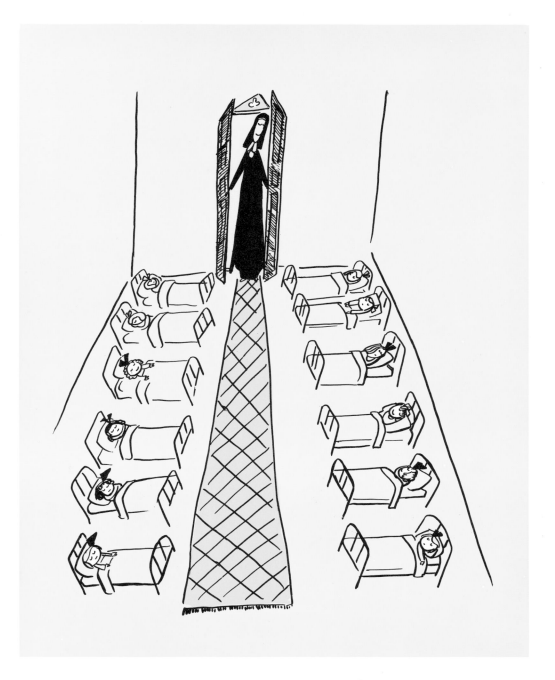

And as Miss Clavel turned out the light
She said, "I knew it would all come out right."

They went home and broke their bread
And brushed their teeth and went to bed,

And Madeline told Pepito that
He was no longer a BAD HAT.
She said, "You are our pride and joy,
You are the world's most wonderful boy!"

The little girls all cried "Boo-hoo!"

But Madeline said, "I know what to do."

Even Miss Clavel said,

"It's too much!"

His love of animals was such,

Went back to their native habitat.

And the starling and turtle, the bunny and bat,

Turned into a Vegetarian.

And lo and behold, the former Barbarian

"I'll never hurt another cat,"
Pepito said. "I swear to that.
I've learned my lesson. Please believe
I'm turning over a new leaf."
"That's fine," she said. "I hope you do.
We all will keep our eyes on you!"

So Madeline went in on tiptoe,
And whispered, "Can you hear me, Pepito?
It serves you right, you horrid brat,
For what you did to that poor cat."

"Only one visitor at a time,
Will you go in first, Miss Madeline?"

The Ambassadress wept tears of joy,
As she thanked Miss Clavel for saving her boy.

"Nothing," said the Ambassador,
"Would cheer up poor Pepito more
Than a visit from next door.

In the Embassy of Spain.

She came in time to save the Bad Hat,
And Madeline took care of the cat.
Good-by, Fido; so long, Rover.
Let's go home—the fun is over.

There was sorrowing and pain

And now just listen to the poor
Boy crying, "AU SECOURS!"
Which you must cry, if by any chance
You're ever in need of help in France.

Miss Clavel ran fast and faster
To the scene of the disaster.

He said, "Let's have a game of tag"—
And let a CAT out of the bag!

There were no trees, and so instead
The cat jumped on Pepito's head.

Look at him bringing those doggies food!"

"That boy is simply misunderstood.

Of all the dogs in the neighborhood.

He was followed by an increasing pack

Pepito carried a bulging sack.

Madeline said, "Oh, look who's there!"

One day, when out to take the air,

He ate them ROASTED, GRILLED, and FRITO!
¡Oh, what a horror was PEPITO!

He was unmoved by the last look
The frightened chickens gave the cook.

He built himself a GUILLOTINE!

"I knew it—listen to him play,
Hammering, sawing, and working away."

Oh, but that boy was really mean!

Said Miss Clavel, "It seems to me
He needs an outlet for his energy.

"A chest of tools might be attractive
For a little boy that's very active.

But in a short while, the little elf
Was back again, and his old self.

Madeline answered, "A Torero
Is not at all our idea of a hero!"
The poor lad left; he was lonesome and blue;
He shut himself in—what else could he do?

He changed his clothes and said, "I bet
This invitation they'll accept."

But Madeline said, "Please don't molest us,
Your menagerie does not interest us."

One day he climbed upon the wall
And cried, "Come, I invite you all!
Come over some time, and I'll let you see
My toys and my menagerie—
My frogs and birds and bugs and bats,
Squirrels, hedgehogs, and two cats.
The hunting in this neighborhood
Is exceptionally good."

And Miss Clavel said, "Isn't he nice!"

He was sure and quick on ice,

Year in, year out, he was polite.

That he flew the highest kite.

In the autumn wind he boasted

On hot summer nights he ghosted;

Causing pain and shocked surprise
During morning exercise.

In the spring when birdies sing
Something suddenly went "zing!"

Madeline said, "It is evident that
This little boy is a Bad Hat!"

His Excellency has a boy.

Look, my darlings, what bliss, what joy!

Moved into the house next door.

One day the Spanish Ambassador

In an old house in Paris
That was covered with vines
Lived twelve little girls
In two straight lines.
They left the house at half-past-nine
In two straight lines, in rain or shine.
The smallest one was Madeline.

PUFFIN BOOKS

A Division of Penguin Books USA Inc.

375 Hudson Street, New York, New York 10014

Penguin Books Ltd, 27 Wrights Lane, London W8 5TZ England

Penguin Books Australia Ltd, Ringwood, Victoria, Australia

Penguin Books Canada Ltd, 10 Alcorn Avenue, Toronto, Ontario, Canada M4V 3B2

Penguin Books (N.Z.) Ltd, 182-190 Wairau Road, Auckland 10, New Zealand

Penguin Books Ltd, Registered Offices: Harmondsworth, Middlesex, England

First published by The Viking Press 1956
Viking Seafarer Edition published 1968
Reprinted 1970, 1972, 1973, 1975
Published in Picture Puffins 1977

30   29

Library of Congress Cataloging in Publication Data
Bemelmans, Ludwig, 1898-1962. Madeline and the bad hat.
Summary: When the Spanish ambassador moves in next door, Madeline
and the rest of the twelve little girls discover that his son
is not the best neighbor.
[1. Stories in rhyme] I. Title.
PZ8.3.B425Mac7 [E] 77-1976
ISBN 0-14-050206-8

Manufactured in the U.S.A.

Set in Bodoni

MADELINE
AND THE BAD HAT

WRITTEN AND ILLUSTRATED BY

Ludwig Bemelmans

PUFFIN BOOKS

MADELINE AND THE BAD HAT

To
Mimi